THAT'S WHEN I'M HAPPY!

Beth Shoshan

Jaqueline East

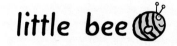

There are some days

when I'm very happy…

and there are some days

when I'm a little bit sad.

But now, on those days

when I'm a little bit sad…

I try and find my way back

to being happy.

When it's cold outside

and my Daddy and I are clearing up...

And when we take a soft striped bag

and fill it up with leaves...

And when he chooses

one special leaf for me

because it's deeper, darker,

redder than all the others...

And when my Daddy

and I play football

through the leaves

and we're kicking

to each other

through a tunnel of trees...

...that's when I'm happy!

When it's cosy inside and my

Mummy and I give each other

great big bear hugs...

And when we rub our noses together...

And when she chooses one

special tickle, just for me

because it's wriggly,

squirmy and makes me laugh

more than all the others...

And then my Mummy

gives me the biggest kiss of all...

And I reach up to give her a big kiss back...

But not as big,

because my mouth is still very small...

...that's when I'm happy!

When it's night outside

and my Daddy and I gaze through the window…

And when he takes my hand

and points at the night sky…

And when he chooses one special star

for me because it's bigger,

burning brighter than all the others…

And then my Daddy

and I count all the stars

in the sky, and he says

there are more than 119...

But I can't count any higher...

...that's when I'm happy!

When it's warm inside and my Mummy

and I run our fingers through the books...

And when we look at all the pictures...

And when she chooses

one special book for me

because it's our favourite,

better than all the others...

And then my Mummy reads

the perfect story to me

and I can read some

of the words...

But mostly the ones

with the letters

from my name in them...

...that's when I'm happy!

When it's dark everywhere

and I cuddle up

to my Mummy and Daddy

(even though they're asleep)

still telling stories to myself,

watching stars in the sky,

bathed in all their kisses

and dreaming of the deep

red leaves...

That's when we're happy!

For Joshua, Asher and Hannah

B.S.

Thanks Vicki

J.E.

First published in 2005
by Meadowside Children's Books
185 Fleet Street, London, EC4A 2HS

This edition published in 2008 by Little Bee
an imprint of Meadowside Children's Books

Text Beth Shoshan
Illustrations © Jaqueline East 2005

The right of Jacqueline East to be identified
as the illustrator of this work
has been asserted by her in accordance with
the Copyright, Designs and Patents Act, 1988

A CIP catalogue record for this book
is available from the British Library
Printed in Malaysia

10 9 8 7 6 5 4